Jillian Jiggs and the Great Big Snow

Phoebe Gilman

North Winds Press
An imprint of Scholastic Canada Ltd.

The paintings for this book were created in gouache and coloured pencils on Arches Watercolour Paper. This book was designed in QuarkXPress, with type set in 16 point American Typewriter.

6 5 4 3 2 1 Printed in Singapore 46 12 13 14 15 16

Library and Archives Canada Cataloguing in Publication

Gilman, Phoebe, 1940-2002
Jillian Jiggs and the great big snow / Phoebe Gilman. -- 10th anniversary ed.

ISBN 978-1-4431-1949-8

I. Title.

PS8563.I54J52 2012 jC813'.54 C2012-901668-3

For two very special people,
Diane Kerner & Yüksel Hassan
XOXO

Silently, silently, all through the night,
Snowflakes had fallen, lacy and white.
By morning the town shimmered brilliant and new,
Promising wonderful, wild things to do.

Jillian Jiggs grabbed her toastiest clothes,
Pulled her woolliest socks up and over her toes,
Put on her sweater, her snow pants, and then,
Looked for her hat. It was missing again.

"Jillian, Jillian, say it's not true.
How do you lose all the things that you do?
You'd lose your head if it wasn't attached.
And where would I find you another that matched?"

"My hat isn't lost. It just hasn't been found.
Look — my scarf's long. I can wrap it around."

“No,” said her mother. “Now go find your hat.
The weather’s too cold to go outside like that.”

Jillian searched every room, everywhere.
It had vanished, gone poof, disappeared in thin air.
She needed a hat and she needed it fast.
There was no time to waste, ’cause the snow might not last.

She opened her toy chest and pulled out some things:
A dragon, a mask and two butterfly wings.
Some boxes, a wand and a Martian hat too . . .

“I can’t find THAT hat, but another might do.”

"What do you think, Mom? Is this hat okay?
Mom . . . did you hear me? Can I go and play?"

Her mother stood up, took a deep breath and said,
"As long as it's warm and it stays on your head."

"Are you ready, Rebecca? Come on now, let's go!
Hop on the sled and we'll play in the snow."

Her friends took one look at the hat on her head:
"It's different," said Rachel. "It's weird," Peter said.

"My old hat is missing. I looked everywhere.
It vanished, went poof, disappeared in thin air.

When I couldn’t find it, I took this instead.
So now I’m a Martian kid,” Jillian said.

"Which means we're on Mars. And the Martians . . . Oh, no! The Martians are stuck underneath all this snow!"

“We’ll save them,” said Peter. “We’re smart and we’re tough. Come on. Let’s get going. Start digging this stuff.”

Little by little, they shovelled it clear,
And an alien landscape began to appear.
It had long, snaking roads and odd-looking hills,
And monsters to give you the shivers and chills.

One kind of creature had eyes on his snout,
And all that you saw was that snout sticking out
Of the door to his house, which was really a cave.
No one explored there unless they were brave.

Peter made one that had spikes on its tail.
Rachel's resembled a two-headed snail.

"My Martian's name is Thing-a-ma-bob.
He's small," said Rebecca, "and shaped like a blob."

"When these are finished they'll be Martian pigs.
I like pigs. They're friendly," said Jillian Jiggs.

"Jillian, Jillian, look, look! It's gone!
Where is the warm, woolly scarf you had on?"

They searched every hill, every cave, everywhere.

It had vanished, gone poof, disappeared in thin air.

"I'm in big trouble. When our mom finds out,
She'll fall down and faint, then she'll wake up and shout:

Jillian, Jillian, say it's not true!
How do you lose all the things that you do?"

“Are you going to stand around moping all day?
Come on now,” said Rachel. “We’re here to play!”

"You're right. Gone is gone," said Jillian Jiggs.
"I'm here on Mars and I'm making snow pigs.
This nose needs improving. It has to be flat."
She poked in pig nostrils. "It's perfect like that."

"Except for one detail," said Jillian Jiggs.
They lifted Rebecca, who added the twigs.

"Jillian, Jillian, look, look! They're gone!
Where are the mittens you used to have on?
You're in big trouble. When our mom finds out,
She'll fall down and faint, then she'll wake up and shout:

> Jillian, Jillian, say it's not true!
> How do you lose all the things that you do?"

They searched every cave, every hill, everywhere.
The mittens had gone, disappeared in thin air.

“Face it,” said Rachel. “It’s not the first time.
Your things just get lost. Don’t stand there and whine.”

Jillian smiled and blew her a kiss.
“My sleeves are long. I’ll wear them like this.”

"I'm ready," said Peter, "to try something new.
I've thought of another neat thing we can do.
We're here on Mars where the hills are so high,
I bet if we try them, our space sleds will fly!"

Peter was right. They zoomed down so fast,
All Mars was a blur as they hurtled past.

Swooping and looping, they dove and they dipped,
Not even stopping when they flopped or flipped.

It was then that her hat disappeared off her head.
"Oh no! Not again," poor Jillian said.

"You're in big trouble. When your mom finds out,
She'll fall down and faint, then she'll wake up and shout:

> Jillian, Jillian, say it's not true!
> How do you lose all the things that you do?"

They climbed up the hill and they searched with great care.
They shook every bush, but the hat wasn't there.

At last they gave up. They admitted defeat.
Besides, they were hungry. They needed to eat.

Jillian worried, "My mom will be mad.
How does it happen? I'm not REALLY bad."

Peter leaned over, whispering low.
"If she doesn't see you, then she'll never know."

"I'll tiptoe, like this, like a small quiet mouse.
She won't see a thing. I'll just sneak in the house."

She opened the door without making a noise,
Tiptoed inside, and then . . .

. . . tripped on her toys.

Her mother came running. “What happened?” she said. And that’s when she noticed her daughter’s bare head.

"Jillian, Jillian, say it's not true!
You've lost your scarf, hat and both mittens, too?
What was it this time? Where did they go?"

“They’re somewhere on Mars and they’re buried in snow!”